Three   Four   Five

Tallulah's Nutcracker

by MARILYN SINGER

Illustrations by

ALEXANDRA BOIGER

CLARION BOOKS

Houghton Mifflin Harcourt | Boston | New York

Clarion Books
215 Park Avenue South, New York, New York 10003

Clarion Books is an imprint of Houghton Mifflin Harcourt Publishing Company.
www.hmhbooks.com

The text was set in Pastonchi MT Std.
The illustrations were executed in watercolor, as well as watercolor mixed with gouache
and egg yolk, on Fabriano watercolor paper.

Library of Congress Cataloging-in-Publication Data
Singer, Marilyn.
Tallulah's Nutcracker / by Marilyn Singer ; illustrated by Alexandra Boiger.
p. cm.
Summary: Tallulah is thrilled to play a mouse in a professional production of
The Nutcracker and works very hard to be the most marvelous mouse of all,
but opening night brings some surprises.
ISBN 978-0-547-84557-9 (hardcover)
[1. Ballet dancing—Fiction. 2. Nutcracker (Choreographic work)
—Fiction. 3. Christmas—Fiction.] I. Boiger, Alexandra, ill. II. Title.
PZ7.S6172Taf 2013
[Fic]—dc23
2012034744

Manufactured in China
SCP 10 9 8 7 6 5 4 3 2 1
4500418403

To Jennifer Greene, who sent Tallulah to ballet school!
—M.S.

To Jennifer Greene, Marcia Wernick,
and Marilyn Singer, with love and respect.
Fröhliche Weihnachten!
—A.B.

THERE was only one Christmas present that Tallulah *really* wanted. When the phone rang, she was sure her wish had come true—and she was right.

"They picked me!" she shouted. "I'm going to be a mouse in *The Nutcracker*. Lots of kids tried out, but they picked ME!"

"I thought you wanted to be the Sugar Plum Fairy. You said you didn't want to be a mouse, ever," said her brother, Beckett. He *loved* being a mouse.

"That was in our dance school." Tallulah sniffed. "This is a *real* Nutcracker for a *real* ballet company in a *real* theater."

"Can I come see it?"

"Of course you can! Lots of people will come!" Tallulah exclaimed.

"And everybody will get to see ME dance!"

In ballet class, all the students congratulated Tallulah.

"What wonderful news!" said her teacher, giving her a hug.

"It's a great honor!"

"I know it is," Tallulah agreed, doing chaîné turns around the room.

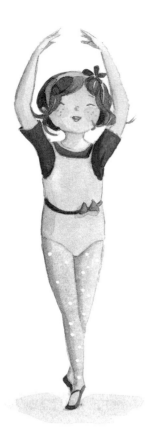

That day, she worked extra hard. She turned out her hips and feet in a fabulous fifth position and rose on her toes in a splendid sous-sus.

Then she jumped to one foot in a graceful sissonne. **Ballet class is fun,** she thought, **but being in a real ballet is Big Time. Maybe I'll be on TV!** Tallulah could hardly wait.

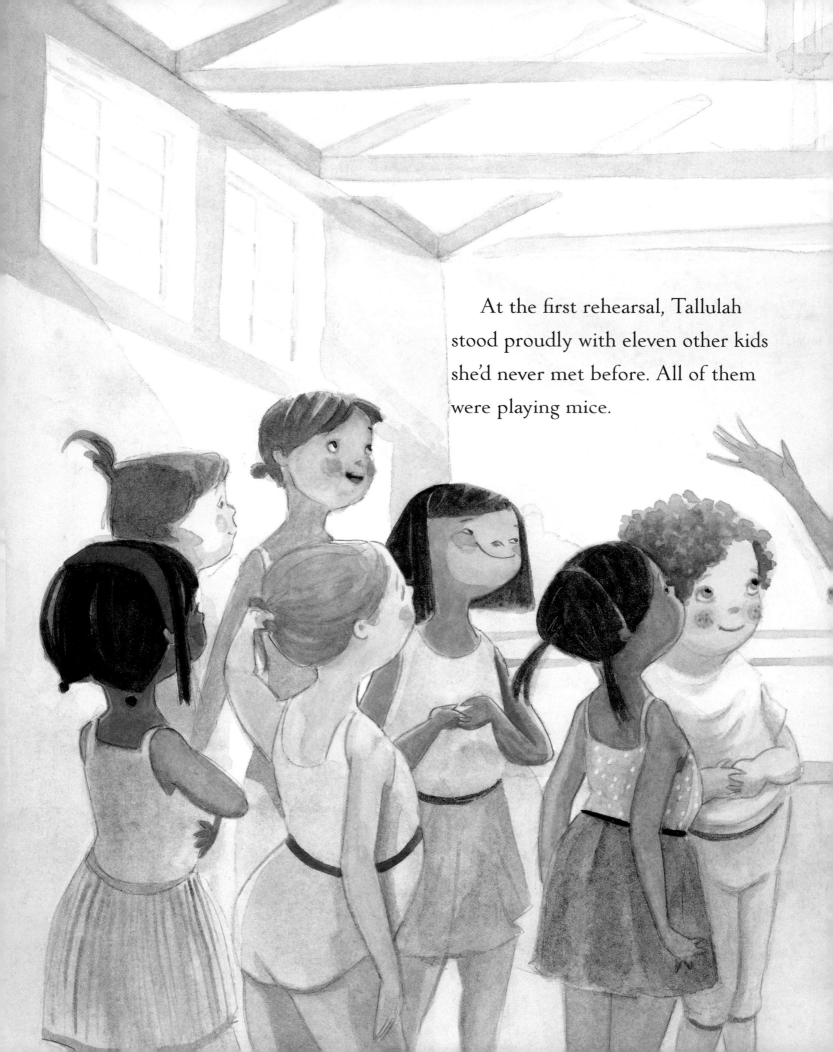

At the first rehearsal, Tallulah stood proudly with eleven other kids she'd never met before. All of them were playing mice.

Tallulah hoped that she would stand out.
The ballet master greeted them warmly.

Then he told them the story of *The Nutcracker:* A girl named Clara receives a nutcracker shaped like a soldier for Christmas, and her jealous brother breaks it. That night, she has a dream about scary mice battling toy soldiers. "That's where you come in," said the ballet master. He showed them a hoop. "Let's pretend that this is the clock you mice come through. Are we ready to begin?"

"Yes!" everyone called back.
Tallulah's voice was loudest of all.

The ballet master lined them up and made
them creep through the pretend clock.

He made them scuttle in a circle and run this way and that.

Then he made them do it all over again.

And again.

Tallulah paid careful attention and did
just what she was told. She didn't get to do
a sous-sus or a sissonne. She didn't even do a plié.
She mostly scurried around, wiggling her paws.
She was starting to feel tired.

But when the dance master said, "Good work, Tallulah. You're a very scary mouse," she beamed. **The whole audience will notice me, too. I bet they'll ask for my autograph.**

With a burst of energy, she lined up at the clock for the fourth time.

Tallulah went to many rehearsals.
She didn't have time to go Christmas
tree shopping with her family or catch
the season's first snowflakes on her tongue.

When a girl in her dance class asked her to a holiday party, Tallulah told her, "I'm sorry, but I'm way too busy. That's the same day as our dress rehearsal." She raised her voice so that all the girls in the dressing room could hear. "I'm in *The Nutcracker,* you know." She was more than ready for Opening Night.

The theater was packed. Everyone Tallulah knew was in the audience. There were even TV cameras.

Tallulah stood in a backstage room with the other mice. The glittering Sugar Plum Fairy was stretching in one corner. Clara was in another. They both looked elegant.

Tallulah stretched a little, too. She was wearing a gray jumpsuit, ears, whiskers, and a tail. She did not look elegant. But she decided that it didn't matter.

Tonight I am a mouse, but soon I'll be Clara, then the Sugar Plum Fairy. The most elegant Sugar Plum Fairy ever!

"Mice! Toy soldiers! Places!"
called the stage manager.

Tallulah hurried to the wings. She watched as
Clara fell asleep. The music got a little spooky.
Tallulah's stomach started to dance by itself.
She took a deep breath and gave it a little pat.
Then, right on cue, as Clara's dream began,
she crept out of the clock with the other
mice behind her. "Ooh," said the audience.
Tallulah was pretty sure that Beckett's
ooh was the loudest.

She took a look at the crowd and gulped.

But she reminded herself, **I'm the scariest, mousiest, most marvelous mouse of all,** and with a fierce twitch of her whiskers, she began to dance.

Then all of a sudden she stepped on a tall mouse's tail.

Whomp! They both fell down.

Tallulah tried to get up, but another mouse tripped over her, followed by two toy soldiers. They all lay in a stunned heap in the middle of the stage.

The audience gasped—then giggled. Tallulah wished she could disappear through the floor. With her face as pink as the inside of her mouse ears, she managed to scramble to her feet. She finished her dance in a daze.

Then she rushed offstage and hid.

Afterward, Tallulah didn't want to face anyone. She sat alone in a backstage room with tears rolling down her cheeks. **I thought I was going to be the best mouse, but I was the total worst,** she said to herself. **I thought I was better than everyone else, but they're all better than me. I'm never going to be a star.**

She was rubbing her eyes when the dance master came in. Clara was with him, and, to Tallulah's great surprise, so was the Sugar Plum Fairy.

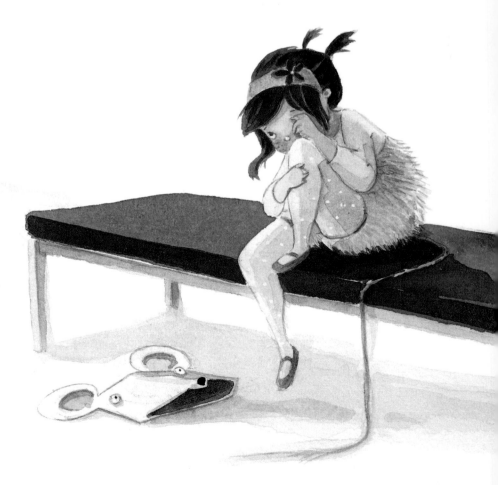

The dance master sat down next to Tallulah, handed her a handkerchief, and put an arm around her shoulders. "When I was your age, I played a party guest in *The Nutcracker*. We drank real punch. Someone put ginger ale in it. I burped loud enough for the whole audience to hear."

Tallulah blinked. "Really?" she said.

"Really," replied the dance master.

"Two years ago I played a snowflake," said Clara.
"I forgot to take off my pink and green striped legwarmers.
The audience couldn't stop giggling."

Tallulah blew her nose. "Oh, no!" she exclaimed.

Then she looked at the Sugar Plum Fairy.

"Last year I was the Flower Queen. I did a lovely
pirouette—and my skirt fell off."

Tallulah couldn't help it—she started to laugh.
The Sugar Plum Fairy joined in.

"You know, Tallulah," said the dance master, "in ballet, embarrassing things happen all the time, but a REAL dancer keeps right on dancing. And that's just what you did . . .

"Now, come on and say hello to your fans." He led her out to where her family and friends were waiting.

They all hugged her. Beckett hugged her hardest of all.

As they
walked out of the
theater, Tallulah thought,
**Well, maybe I'm not
the best mouse or a star,
but I AM a real dancer—
at least, I'm going to be.**

"Merry Christmas!" she hollered.

"It's not Christmas yet," Beckett said, confused.

"For me it is," Tallulah replied, and, with a grin, she stood high on her toes, wiggling her mouse paws in the frosty December air.

Sissonne (see-SAWN)

One

Two

Three

Dinosaur School

WHICH IS DIFFERENT?

Please visit our website, www.garethstevens.com. For a free color catalog of all our high-quality books, call toll free 1-800-542-2595 or fax 1-877-542-2596.

Publisher Cataloging Data

Jeffries, Joyce
      Which is different? – 1st ed. / by Joyce Jeffries.
p.   cm. – (Dinosaur school)
Summary: Colorful dinosaurs introduce sorting.
ISBN 978-1-4339-8103-6 (hard bound) – ISBN 978-1-4339-8104-3 (pbk.)
ISBN 978-1-4339-8105-0 (6-pack)
      1. Set theory—Juvenile literature   [1. Set theory] I. Title
         2013
    511.3/22—dc23

First Edition

Published in 2013 by
Gareth Stevens Publishing
111 East 14th Street, Suite 349
New York, NY 10003

Copyright © 2013 Gareth Stevens Publishing

Designer: Mickey Harmon
Editor: Katie Kawa

All illustrations by Planman Technologies

Printed in the United States of America

CPSIA compliance information: Batch #CW13GS: For further information contact Gareth Stevens, New York, New York at 1-800-542-2595.

WHICH IS DIFFERENT?

By Joyce Jeffries

 Gareth Stevens
Publishing

Which is different?

The orange is different.

Which is different?

The hat is different.

Which is different?

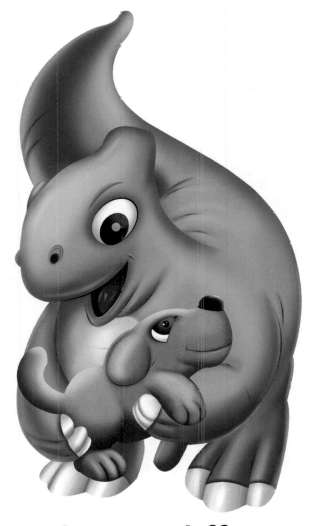

The dog is different.

Which is different?

The book is different.

Which is different?

The shoes are different.

Which is different?

The ice cream is different.

Which is different?

The tricycle is different.

Which is different?

The fish is different.

Which is different?

The dress is different.

Which is different?

The kite is different.

Which is different?